The Lost Voice

Cynthia Rider • Alex Brychta

OXFORD
UNIVERSITY PRESS

Chip didn't feel very well. His throat
was sore and he couldn't talk.

"Chip has lost his voice," said Dad.

"Oh no!" thought Floppy.

Mum took Chip to the doctor.
Dad took Biff and Kipper to school.
Floppy was all on his own.

"Chip has lost his voice," he
thought sadly. "I wish I could help
him."

"I know!" thought Floppy. "I'll go and find Chip's voice. I'm good at finding things."

He wagged his tail
and ran upstairs.

Floppy ran into Chip's bedroom. He looked under the bed. He found a ball, a toy car, a sticky sweet and a dusty sock . . .

. . . but he didn't find
Chip's lost voice.

Floppy looked in the toy box.
He found lots of toys and lots
of books . . .

. . . but he didn't find
Chip's lost voice.

Suddenly, the phone rang.
"There are voices in the phone,"
thought Floppy. "I bet Chip's voice
is in there."

Floppy hit the phone with his paw.
CRASH! It fell down. A voice said,
"Hello! Is anyone there?"

But it wasn't Chip's voice.

Floppy looked at the radio. "There
are voices in the radio," he thought.
"I bet Chip's voice is in there."

He hit the radio with his paw.
Nothing happened. He hit it harder
. . . and **harder!**

CRASH! The radio fell over
and someone started to sing.

"What a horrible noise," thought
Floppy. "That isn't Chip."

"I bet Chip's voice is in the
television," thought Floppy. He ran
to look. His paw hit the switch and
the television came on.

Floppy saw a dog on the television.
It ran out of a shop with a big bone.

"Wow! That bone looks good,"
thought Floppy.

The dog ran faster and faster. A
voice shouted, "Stop! Stop that dog!"

"That isn't Chip," thought Floppy,
and he went back upstairs.

Floppy saw Teddy on Kipper's bed.
"Teddy!" he thought. "I bet Teddy
has got Chip's voice."

Floppy shook Teddy hard.
Grrrrrrr! growled Teddy.
"Help!" barked Floppy. He dropped
Teddy and ran into Biff's bedroom.

WHOOSH! Floppy went skidding across the floor.

CRASH! Biff's clock fell over. "Wake up!" it shouted.

Floppy was scared. He hid under
Chip's bed and shut his eyes. Soon,
he was fast asleep.

Chip came home. He was feeling a lot better now.

"Where are you, Floppy?" he called.

Floppy jumped up. "Chip has found his voice!" he thought.

He wagged his tail and ran downstairs.

Just then, Biff came in. Her throat
was sore and she couldn't talk.

"Biff has lost her voice," said Dad.

"Oh no!" thought Floppy.

Hidden words

Help Floppy to get his bone by finding the words hidden
within the words on the stairs, like this: h**is**

sticky

crash

Biff

growl

clock

shout

stop

has

his

**Useful common words repeated in this story and other
books in the series.** are came couldn't didn't find
found harder isn't over saw talk thought under
upstairs with
Names in this story: Mum Dad Biff Chip Kipper
Floppy